This book is dedicated to everyone who has ever laughed at their own trumps!

Also, special thanks to my sister, Lynn, for the hours spent co-editing, travelling by train between London and Liverpool.

And thanks to Kate for all the finishing touches.

LITTLE TIGER PRESS
An imprint of Magi Publications
1 The Coda Centre, 189 Munster Road, London SW6 6AW
www.littletigerpress.com

First published in Great Britain 2004

2 4 6 8 10 9 7 5 3 1

Text and illustrations © David Roberts 2004
David Roberts has asserted his right to be identified
as the author and illustrator of this work under the
Copyright, Designs and Patents Act, 1988
All rights reserved

A CIP catalogue record for this book is available
from the British Library

Printed in Belgium by Proost NV

ISBN 1 84506 010 5

POOH!
IS THAT YOU, BERTIE?

David Roberts

LITTLE TIGER PRESS
London

This is Bertie.
He likes making smells.

At the dentist Bertie let off a little poot.
It ponged.

POOT

"POOH!

IS THAT YOU, BERTIE?

That's not polite,"
sniffed Mum.

PARP

Bertie let off a big parp in the art gallery and giggled. No one else did. It ponged.

"POOH!

IS THAT YOU, BERTIE?

I've never been so embarrassed,"
sniffed Dad.

At the café Bertie let off a smelly boff.
It ponged worse than a bad egg.

"POOH!

IS THAT YOU, BERTIE?

It's not nice to break wind in the café,
not when people are eating,"
sniffed Gran.

Bertie let rip a tremendous trump in big sister Suzy's playhouse. It ponged. Suzy was livid.

"POOH!

IS THAT YOU, BERTIE?

You stink, smelly pants,"
sniffed Suzy.

It's not fair! thought Bertie.
I'm not the only one who stinks.

When Mum lets off a poot, she coughs
at the same time to cover it up.

When Dad lets off he's so sneaky...

you don't know what's coming
until it hits you.

Gran's always letting rip.
She just blames the cat.

Suzy claims she never trumps.
But she sounds like a brass band
when she thinks no one's listening!

PRRRRP

FRRRP

PARP

TRUMP

And when the dog boffs,
he wafts it about!

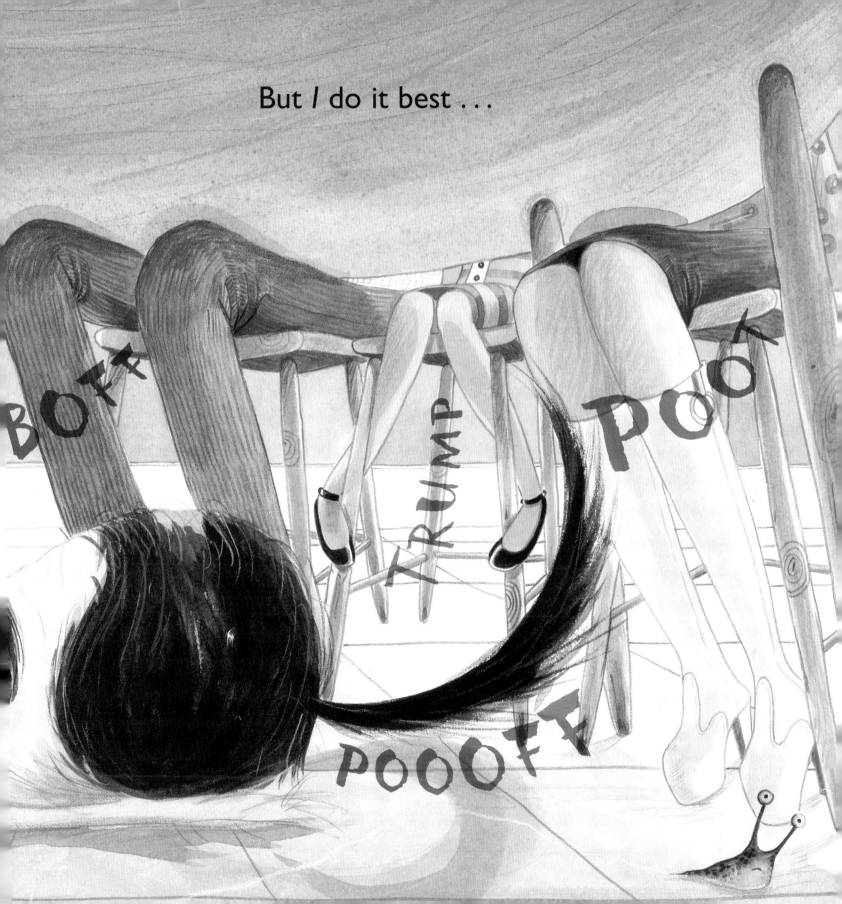

Especially in the bath!

FRRRP